Cold Comforts

An Almanack of the Best and Worst of Britain's Weather

Compiled by
Richard Mabey

Hutchinson
London Melbourne Sydney Auckland Johannesburg

Hutchinson & Co. (Publishers) Ltd

An imprint of the Hutchinson Publishing Group

17–21 Conway Street, London W1P 6JD

Hutchinson Group (Australia) Pty Ltd
30–32 Cremorne Street, Richmond South, Victoria 3121
PO Box 151, Broadway, New South Wales 2007

Hutchinson Group (NZ) Ltd
32–34 View Road, PO Box 40-086, Glenfield, Auckland 10

Hutchinson Group (SA) Pty Ltd
PO Box 337, Bergvlei 2012, South Africa

First published 1983
© Richard Mabey 1983

Set in Linotron Sabon by
Rowland Phototypesetting Ltd
Bury St Edmunds, Suffolk

Printed in Great Britain by The Anchor Press Ltd
and bound by Wm Brendon & Son Ltd,
both of Tiptree, Essex

Preface

As these things often turn out, I am writing this introduction in the middle of the second most spectacular heatwave England has experienced since the war. Yesterday there were snowploughs out in Yorkshire, spreading sand over the melting roads; and in my neighbouring town, Hemel Hempstead, the municipal dahlia beds caught fire when someone dropped a cigarette end onto ground that had turned into a dried-out cake of inflammable fertilizer.

Such bizarre occurrences are nothing new, as the quickest glance through this almanack of two centuries of our capricious weather will show. What is odd about our national obsession with the weather is how forgetful we are, how unimaginative, how *apologetic*, as if climate were something marginal to the business of real life. Yet after a fortnight of temperatures reaching into the 90s, I don't think there can be much doubt about which of the great events of our time people would currently regard as most closely affecting them. Mortgage-rate bickering and party-leadership battles are a distant foreign babble, beyond the ken of parkbench and deckchair (just as the economic depression was dwarfed by those other lows driving incessantly in from the Atlantic during the dripping spring of 1983). Lager stocks are already on ration and television sets on the blink. And in the unemployment desert of the Midlands a man has just chosen to be sacked rather than change out of his shorts. Tomorrow someone may even get round to producing an English translation for *mañana*.

Of course we should be obsessed with the weather. It is one of the great forces that shape our lives, and one of the few we all experience in common. Weather is a great leveller – and a great raiser, too, on the rare occasions it turns out to be indisputably fine.

But heatwaves, like all prolonged extremes, are something of an exception. Our problem is that we have a temperamental climate and a way of talking about it to match – more tetchy gossip than real conversation. Our memories for weather are so short and unreliable that we have no real sense of what it was like even in the recent past, and we fuss so irritably about inaccurate forecasts and bleak outlooks that we rarely bother to appreciate what is happening now. I don't think we really *know* our weather (and I'm not talking about making sense of all the jargon about 'occluded fronts' and 'blocking anticyclones'), how deeply it affects us, and that it has a history that is inextricably entwined with our own.

I compiled *Cold Comforts* – an anthology of past weathers – as a small gesture towards rebuilding a climatic folk memory. I felt it might be both interesting and reassuring to be able to see, almost day by day, that even the most savage downpours and interminable droughts have all happened before, and that we have not only managed to survive but have even contrived to enjoy some of it. As far back as records go, floods and freeze-ups have played havoc with the fragile settlements we continue to build in the obstinate belief that we have a stable climate; they have tormented hill sheep and rheumatic pensioners, precipitated strikes and sent the cost of living soaring. And, simultaneously, the astonishing, unpredictable variety of our climate (which is its most endearing and dangerous feature) has inspired some of our finest descriptive writing and painting. So I have tried to blend anonymous meteorological records of waterspouts, ice-meteors and downpours of frozen birds with some of the vivid observations of our great diarists: notably the Rev. Francis Kilvert, on the Welsh border; Dorothy Wordsworth, fretting about whether the enervating Lake District gales would bring on another of William's migraines; and Gilbert White, the eighteenth-century naturalist-parson from Hampshire. He is my favourite, so I make no apologies for including a good deal of him. The meticulous weather notes he kept over nearly forty years not only have the spare clarity of a haiku, but were also written during a period of climatic instability uncannily like our own. No one can read any of these records without feeling a great rush of recognition and relief: we aren't alone, out there in the drizzle.

These actual histories, preserved both in records and in literature, make our repeated, rather dumbstruck surprise whenever the weather does anything slightly out of the ordinary (and our complaints when it does not) all the more curious. To hear us talk you would think that any slightly exceptional disturbances of the atmosphere were not only un-British but unnatural. Every time we have a real winter or a long heatwave we marvel at our national helplessness, but fail utterly to be prepared the next time.

We can't really excuse ourselves because of truly overpowering conditions. By the standards of most of the rest of the world our climate is positively benign. Volcanic eruptions, major earthquakes, and monsoons are unkown. The temperature has only exceeded 100°F three times this century. The heaviest single rainfall in a single day was 9.56 inches (in Bruton, Somerset, on 28 June 1917) and you have only to compare that figure with the several feet that can fall in a few hours in a tropical downpour to get our weather into perspective. I suspect that the problems we have with our weather have less to do with its occasional excesses than with its regular changeability. As an eccentrically shaped island, stuck in the middle of the Storm Belt, just offshore from a huge continental land mass, Britain's meteorological lot is a turbulent and unpredictable one, whether we like it or not. Of course there are exceptions. One thing I hope this little book will bring out is how often similar weather happens on identical dates in different years – not every year but more often than would be expected by chance. There are a few reliable periods, too: gales and storms are virtually inevitable in the first week of January, and fine weather in the second week of May, for example.

But by and large our weather is such that we haven't much hope of ever becoming acclimatized (literally, for once), and the social impact of this is enormous. Farmers, housebuilders and holiday-makers all take daily climatic gambles, and have suffered frequent and devastating setbacks, as can be seen repeatedly in the following pages.

But what is less appreciated (at least officially) is the extent to which these shifting patterns of weather affect our mood, behaviour and even basic physiological processes. We have all been 'under the weather' on occasions, irritable when it is stuffy, nauseous in thunderstorms, perhaps; and research work in Europe has shown that there is scarcely a single bodily process that isn't affected by changes in the temperature, humidity, pressure and the electrical charge of the atmosphere. Temperature influences the width of blood vessels and the rate at which many hormones are secreted. Changes in humidity affect the permeability of mucous membranes to germs. Electrically charged air can stimulate the production of chemicals that are involved in triggering migraines and asthma. The most bizarre collection of symptoms occur during the passage of a front, when almost every kind of human affliction from appendicitis to phantom limb pain shows a dramatic increase in incidence.

So it would seem that we in Britain do suffer more keenly at the hands of the weather than those in more stable climates. In a country where you can guarantee three months of ice and snow every winter, you can design your lifestyle to cope with this. We, on the other hand, have to make the best of whatever turns up. And just as we have begun to adapt, some new weather pattern is invariably on the way.

There's very little we can do about this, yet we make things worse by going to the most extraordinary lengths to avoid confronting and accepting our natural weather. We blame jumbo jets and satellites. We blame last year's mild winter for this year's bad summer, and with a typical piece of national pessimism, expect we'll 'have to pay for it' when we do have a good spell. In something very close to voodoo we even blame the weather forecasters themselves, who, having seen the awesome complexity of the weather system with their new technology, wisely get more vague and tentative by the day.

How much more comforting it would be if instead of all this anxious peering forwards, we looked back for once, and saw that throughout our history the good and bad spells have always balanced themselves out; that even at its worst, weather is rarely unmitigatedly ugly, and has repeatedly brought out acts of heroism, humour and imagination in our people. And at its best it can be breathtakingly beautiful. Where else in the world could you experience, in the course of a few weeks, snow rollers, a glazed frost, snowdrops flowering under a flood and a halo round the moon? The British climate is part of our national heritage, and the next time we are tempted to complain, we should remember those expatriate Britishers, trapped in a Singapore monsoon or an Australian drought who are at that moment pining for the 'occasional showers' of home.

A few words about the organization and sources of the material. I have chosen the entries not just to give examples of record and extreme weather (what they called 'meteors' in the eighteenth century) but

Preface

also typical days, and I have, here and there, tried to bring out both continuity and contrast in the patterns for particular times of the year.

Many of the stories come from a file of newspaper clippings I have been keeping in an informal way for the last twelve years, but I have also borrowed freely from a large range of books. I would especially like to acknowledge *Weather*, the journal of the Royal Meteorological Society; Gordon Manley's superb New Naturalist volume, *Climate and the British Scene* (Collins); Ingrid Holdford's *British Weather Disasters* (David and Charles) and *The Guinness Book of Weather Facts and Feats* (Guinness Superlatives Ltd); *Dry Humour* (The National Water Council); *Kilvert's Diary*, edited by William Plomer (Cape); *Home at Grasmere* (Dorothy Wordsworth's journals) edited by Collette Clark (Penguin); *Gerard Manley Hopkins Poems and Prose*, ed. W. H. Gardner (Penguin); Gilbert White's journals in the British Museum (and the selection edited by Walter Johnson, republished by David and Charles); and the anthology *The English Year* compiled by Geoffrey Grigson (Oxford).

Extracts from journals are all credited with their authors' names and the place where they were written. A few extracts from my own diary are initialled RM.

Given the very wide variety of sources, from poetic and popular to scientific, I have made no attempt to regularize the units of measurement, but give them as they were set down by the original observer.

Richard Mabey, Berkhamsted, July 1983

January

'I said it's astonishing how quiet these resorts are in the winter'

1st 1979 Storm all night. The may-pole is blown down. Thatch and tiles damaged.

Gilbert White (Selborne)

2nd/3rd 1976 Hurricane-force gales across Britain overnight, with gusts in excess of 100 m.p.h. in many parts of East Anglia, reaching 134 m.p.h. at Lowther Hill, Lanarkshire and 76 m.p.h. at Holborn in central London. At one stage every road out of Norwich was blocked by fallen trees, and nationwide the damage was reckoned to be as severe as during the great storm of 1703 (see p. 71). (I noted in my own diary that 'at midnight the foliage of our churchyard yew was streaming sideways like bunting caught in a fan.' R.M.)

2nd 1886   Cold weather brings out upon the faces of people the written marks of their habits, vices, passions, and memories, as warmth brings out on a paper a writing in sympathetic ink.

Thomas Hardy (Dorset)

3rd 1978   A swarm of tornadoes struck East Anglia. The whole of Norfolk was enveloped by snow, hail, gale-force winds and electrical storms of such ferocity that 136 pink-footed geese were literally knocked dead out of the sky. It was thought at first that they had been struck by lightning, but autopsies on a sample showed extensive lung and liver damage more likely to have been due to pressure effects in the heart of the tornado.

3rd 1979   'Snow-rollers' (natural snowballs formed by strong winds passing over wet, slightly melting snow) seen up to 7 inches in diameter in Lincolnshire.

4th 1979   Southeasterly gales drove the sea into the Devon coastal resorts of Torcross and Beesands, with huge boulders being tossed into the streets by 30-foot waves.

5th 1804   I distinctly and repeatedly saw the wind raise up from the mountain a true genuine cloud of snow, that rose high . . . sailed along, a true genuine large white cloud with all the form and varied outline of a cloud – and this in several instances dropped again, snow at second hand, and often in the sun resembled a shower of diamond spearlets.

Samuel Coleridge (Lake District)

5th 1941 A pearly opalescence (caused by soot particles suspended in the lower atmosphere after stormy weather) was visible over Kinder Scout from Manchester, 10 miles away.

6th 1879 Old Christmas Day. Last night the slip of the Holy Thorn . . . grafted for me last spring in the Vicarage Lower Garden, blossomed in an intense frost.

Francis Kilvert (Herefordshire)

6th 1928 London flooded, after a thaw of deep, Christmas snow. The Tate Gallery was flooded up to the ceiling of the ground floor, and many canvases of that incomparable painter of English weather, Turner, were submerged (but subsequently rescued and restored). The Tower of London moats flowed with water again, and the floods also reached Lots power station, Wandsworth gasworks, Temple station and the Blackwall Tunnel.

8th/9th 1982 Start of the severest snowstorms of the 1982 winter. Blizzards raged for 48 hours without cease in Wales and much of the West Country, and as much as 2 feet of snow fell in places. The police closed off the slip-roads onto the M4 and M5 by rolling giant snowballs across the carriageways. Simultaneously, temperatures fell to record lows – below -20°C in many places. Fish in nets froze rigid as they were pulled out of the sea in Scotland,

and a motorist in Perth was found with his lips frozen to his car door-handle. Despite the extreme temperatures, this was a short-lived severe winter, and a thaw set in on 15 January.

9th 1973   An ice meteor (a piece of ice falling from the sky, with no obvious origin) smashed a porch at West Wickham, Kent. It weighed 10 lb.

9th 1982   A thousand people rescued from stranded cars in Wales.

9th 1982   The A41 almost impassable to traffic, and many people doing weekend shopping with toboggans. They are parked in little rows alongside the supermarket trolleys.

R.M. (Herts.)

10th 1974   An exceptionally low pressure front brought severe gales and storms to southern England. The temperature dropped 11°F in half-an-hour and hailstones up to 1 inch across were being driven by winds gusting over 90 m.p.h.

10th 1982   The coldest temperature ever recorded in Britain: -27.2°C (-17°F) in Braemar.

10th 1971   The highest January temperature ever: 65°F in Aber, Gwynedd.

11th 1978   Severe gales in England, gusting up to 95 m.p.h. at Tynemouth. Piers were damaged or destroyed at Margate, Skegness, Hunstanton and Herne Bay.

12th 1969   A light vessel off Cork recorded a wave height of 42 feet, more than four times the average.

13th 1930   70 m.p.h. gusts recorded in the heart of Kensington.

14th 1776   Rugged, Siberian weather. The narrow lanes are full of snow in some places, which is driven into most romantic, and grotesque shapes. The road-waggons are obliged to stop, and the stagecoaches are much embarrassed. I was obliged to be much abroad on this day, and scarce ever saw its fellow.

Gilbert White (Selborne)

15th 1982   Snow and ground still frozen iron-hard. Small birds roosting on the tarmacked roads at midnight.

R.M. (Herts.)

15th 1968   Storms rage across the whole of Britain. Severe flooding in the south, and in the North Sea the oil rig *Sea Quest* broke loose from her moorings. Glasgow was struck by a tornado, and 100,000 homes were damaged. During the storms the highest mean wind speed over an hour was recorded at Great Dun Fell in Cumbria, 99 m.p.h. (equalling that from Lowther Hill, Scotland on 20 January 1963), with gusts up to 134 m.p.h.

15th 1975   In an exceptionally mild winter, daffodils bloomed at Hampton Court.

16th 1955   Almost total darkness at noon in central London, presaging a snowstorm.

17th 1974   9.37 inches of rain on Loch Sloy, Dunbarton, Scotland's record rainfall for a single day.

18th–21st 1881   One of the greatest snowstorms on record for southern England produced drifts 15 feet deep in Oxford Circus.

19th 1982   Three sheep were rescued alive near Evesham after being buried for 12 days in 15-foot snowdrifts.

20th   1966   Freezing rain caused chaos on roads and railway lines in the south. Because of the ice coating the rails, trains moved in jerks and starts as circuits broke and shorted out. One train welded itself to the conductor rail.

20th 1775   Mr Hool's man says that he caught this day in a lane near Hackwood-park, many rooks, which attempting to fly fell from the trees with their wings frozen together by the sleet, that froze as it fell.
Gilbert White (Selborne)

20th 1776   Fierce frost, sun. . . . Hares, compelled by hunger, come into my garden, and eat the pinks. Lambs fall, and are frozen to the ground.
Gilbert White (Selborne)

20th 1947   Blizzards marked the real beginning of the severe winter of 1947. (There had been premonitory falls of heavy snow after Christmas, and on 4 and 5 January.) By the 30th there was an almost continuous blanket of snow at least 12 inches deep over the whole of England. February brought no improvement with persistently low temperatures, dull skies and biting winds. There was the usual crop of cold weather curiosities. Frozen herring gulls dropped out of the sky in Norfolk, and in Derbyshire the driver of a locomotive was knocked out when his train crashed into a giant icicle in a tunnel. More tragically, 4 million sheep and lambs and 30,000 cattle perished.

This was certainly the snowiest of recent severe winters. Snow fell somewhere in Britain every day between 22 January and 17 March, with many daily falls in excess of 2 feet, and most places had at least 45 days of snow cover. When the thaw came it was rapid, speeded up by warm rains, and the sudden release of countless millions of tons of frozen water caused disastrous flooding, especially in East Anglia.

22nd 1789 Now the ice is melted on Hartley-park pond, many dead fish come floating ashore, which were stifled under the ice for want of air.

Gilbert White (Selborne)

23rd 1972 A block of ice more than 3 feet square fell to earth at Shirley, Surrey.

23rd 1979 Freezing rain fell over a large area of southern England. As raindrops hit window panes they made distinctive ringing noises, and froze on impact to give up to 4mm of glaze.

26th 1902   Red rain fell at Menheniot Vicarage in Cornwall. 'Red deposit came down in heavy rain during a funeral here and stained the open books and white surplices of the choir', a villager noted.

26th 1940   A severe snowstorm on the western flank of the Pennines buried a southbound express train for 36 hours near Preston.

26th 1978   The end of a blizzard which had lasted 50 hours in Scotland.

26th 1979   Norfolk. Yet more snow. The landscape drained of colour and horizons: the white in the fields, the hoar frost on the trees and hedges, and a great bowl of freezing fog. 0°F in places at midnight.

R.M. (Norfolk)

27th 1940   The most infamous and severe ice storm of the century. Rain falling onto a landscape locked under air at sub-zero temperatures froze the instant it touched a solid object, and within a matter of hours the entire countryside appeared to have been crystallized in glass. Cats were iced to branches, birds killed in flight by their wings freezing solid, and ponies on Plynlimon in Wales were frozen to death inside coffins of ice. The weight of ice was such that tree branches which had bent towards the ground became welded in that position, whilst their glazed leaves rattled together like castanets. Telegraph wires rotated under their burden of ice (one stretch in Gloucestershire carried 11¼ tons between just two posts) until they were bizarrely adorned with upward pointing icicles.

29th 1776 An intense frost usually befalls in Jan: our Saxon fore-fathers call'd that month with no small propriety wolf-month; because the severe weather brought down those ravenous beasts out of the woods among the villages.

Gilbert White (London)

29th 1978 A man was rescued after his car had been buried under snow for 80 hours in the Highlands. He was a 68-year-old clothing salesman and had survived by wrapping himself up in dozens of pairs of women's tights, and boring a breathing hole through the snow with his starting handle.

31st–1 Feb 1953 A great storm surge in the North Sea caused the most appalling loss of life and widespread damage to property ever recorded for this kind of weather disaster. The surge resulted when an already high tide was piled up and held inside the narrow funnel between eastern England and the Continent by fierce northerly gales. Ferocious tidal surges, as much as 7 to 10 feet above the normal highest levels, smashed through the sea defence walls in 1200 places along 1000 miles of coast between Spurn Head and Kent. The human consequences were unprecedentedly tragic: 307 people lost their lives, 58 by drowning. The whole population of Canvey Island had to be evacuated, and in all 24,000 houses were flooded and damaged. Gasworks, power stations, railways, sewage works and fresh water supplies were all severely disrupted, and

160,000 acres of farmland were inundated by the salt water. It was nearly four years before normal growing could be resumed in some areas.

But as always there were stories of traditional British stoicism. Amongst the many plaques on East Anglian walls which mark the height of the 1953 floods is one by the fireplace in the bar of the Jolly Sailors, Orford. At the height of the flood the landlord was diving down to the cellar to rescue the beer, which the customers drank sitting with their legs up on the tables.

February

1st 1776   Snow now lying on the roofs for 26 days! Thames frozen above and below bridge: crowds of people running about on the ice. The streets strangely encumbered with snow, which crumbles and treads and looks like bay salt – Carriages run without any noise or clatter.

Gilbert White (London)

1st 1799   I don't know that I ever felt a more severe day. The turnips all froze to blocks, obliged to split them with beetle and wedges, and some difficulty to get at them on account of the snow – their tops entirely gone and they lay as apples on the ground.

Parson Woodforde (Norfolk)

1st 1814   The last Thames Frost Fair. Thirty days of almost continuous air frost had built up large ice floes in the upper reaches of the Thames. By 30 January these had floated downstream and bonded together enough to block the river near London Bridge. On the first day of February the river was iced solid throughout central London, and walking across became a fashionable and popular pastime. Quite soon large numbers of traders had set up business on the ice, selling snacks and drinks. There were swings and sheep roastings, and printing presses turning out commemorative verses. Music, skating and general promenading went on till late at night.

5th 1771   Warm fog. Grey crows. Creeping mist over the meadows.

Gilbert White (Wilts.)

6th 1814   The Thames began to thaw after a change in the wind, and at high tide the river was ringing to the extraordinary hubbub of colliding ice floes.

7th 1772   The snow has lain on the ground this evening just 21 days; a long period for England!

Gilbert White (Selborne)

8th 1947   The sun shone in England for the first time in 21 days.

9th 1859   At Aberdare, Glamorgan, it rained minnows and sticklebacks, covering an area of about a third of an acre with fish (which must have been sucked up by a vertical whirlwind into the rain clouds).

9th 1870 In the Park [Richmond] in the afternoon the wind was driving little clouds of snow-dust which caught the sun as they rose and delightfully took the eyes: flying up the slopes they looked like breaks of sunlight fallen through ravelled cloud upon the hills . . .

Gerard Manley Hopkins (London)

11th 1982 Red rain fell on southern Britain, blown in from the north African deserts.

11th 1974 Gales: 2000 trees blown down in the New Forest.

12th 1870 The slate slabs of the urinals even are frosted in graceful sprays.

Gerard Manley Hopkins (Surrey)

13th 1879 The baby was baptized in ice which was broken and swimming about in the font.

Francis Kilvert (Radnorshire)

13th 1977 Severe floods in the North, Midlands and East Anglia. In Nottinghamshire, a pike was seen chasing a water rat down a flooded street.

13th 1979 60-foot tidal wave off Dorset coast during storms.

14th 1961 Hot weather and brilliant sunshine. 65°F recorded in Bromley, Kent.

14th 1974   St Valentine's Day. Darkness at noon. At 2 p.m. the sky the colour of seaweed. Yet no storm.

R.M. (Middlesex)

15th 1979   Tenth fall of snow since early January in parts of England. Drifts 7 feet deep in East Anglia.

16th 1868   A perfect, quiet, intensely bright sky with silver, silent clouds all day.

John Ruskin (Surrey)

16th 1962   Atlantic gales blowing across Britain brought gusts up to 177 m.p.h. in coastal areas, and 123 m.p.h. inland at Lowther Hill, Strathclyde. In Sheffield freak turbulence caused by the passage of the westerly airstream over the Pennines caused hurricane-force winds locally. Mean wind speed rose to 75 m.p.h. for several hours gusting to 96 m.p.h., and more than 6000 homes were severely damaged.

16th 1925   The southeast fringes of Dartmoor had 6 feet of snow in fifteen hours – without drifting. This was probably the deepest single day's snowfall to fall in Britain below a 1000-foot elevation. Eye-witnesses described the snow as falling 'as if it were shovelled'.

18th/19th 1978   Severe blizzards in the West Country brought drifts up to 30 feet deep. Most of Devon and Cornwall was completely cut off and Lynton in Devon not reached by rescuers for another 6 days.

21st 1978   Sleet fell overnight onto frozen ground and the whole of southern England became locked in a glazed frost. The West Country was immediately declared a disaster area, and the police prohibited all non-essential traffic movements.

22nd 1979   In the afternoon the sun peeped through in London for the first time in weeks. In Regent Street people stepped off the pavement into the watery beams, laughing with surprise.

R.M. (London)

22nd 1903   Red desert dust fell on England. At Liskeard, in Cornwall, a villager noted 'a thick orange-coloured fog came in off the sea. It was very different from our country white fogs.'

23rd 1768   Great rain. Prodigious floods in Yorkshire, which have swept away all the bridges.

Gilbert White (Selborne)

24th 1873   In the snow flat-topped hillocks and shoulders outlined with wavy edges, ridge below ridge, very like the grain of wood in line and in projection like relief maps. These the wind makes I think and of course drifts, which are in fact snow waves.

Gerard Manley Hopkins (Lancs.)

24th 1947   The Great Yarmouth trawler, *Twinkling Star*, returned from the North Sea with her skipper reporting that hot tea had frozen in cups.

February

25th 1947 An orange fog, heavily laced with industrial pollutants, hung over London, marking the longest spell of continuous frost for a hundred years.

26th 1798 A winter prospect shows every cottage, every farm, and the forms of distant trees, such as in summer have no distinguishing mark.

Dorothy Wordsworth (Somerset)

27th 1857 How misty is England! I have spent four years in a gray gloom.

Nathaniel Hawthorne (Lancs.)

27th 1781 Vast storm. Had the duration of this storm been equal to its strength, nothing could have withstood its fury. As it was, it did prodigious damage. The tiles were blown from the roof of Newton church with such violence, that shivers from them broke the windows of the great farmhouse at rear 30 yds distance.

Gilbert White (Selborne)

28th 1891 Highest February temperature on record: 67°F at Barnstaple and Cambridge.

March

BRITISH CHARACTER
Extraordinary propensity of farmers to grumble

2nd 1963 A family on Dartmoor were rescued after 65 days marooned in their isolated farmhouse.

6th 1875 A sudden and blessed change in the weather, a SW wind, bearing warm rain, and the birds in the garden and orchard singing like mad creatures.

Francis Kilvert (Wilts.)

6th 1967 Fastest recorded wind gust in Britain: 144 m.p.h. at Cairngorms Weather Station (alt: 3525 feet).

March

7th 1786 Snow drifted over hedges, and gates! . . . A starving wigeon settled yesterday in the village, and was taken. Mention is made in the newspaper of several people that have perished in the snow. As Mr Ventris came from Faringdon, the drifted snow, being hard-frozen, bore his weight up to the tops of the stiles. The net hung over the cherry-trees is curiously coated over with ice.

Gilbert White (Selborne)

9th 1774 This was the last day of the wet weather: but the waters were so encreased by this day's deluge, that the most astonishing floods ensued . . . In the night between 8th and 9th a vast fragment of an hanger in the parish of Hawkley [Hants] slipped down; and at the same time several fields below were rifted and torn in a wonderful manner . . . 50 acres of ground were disordered and damaged by this strange accident. The turf of some pastures were driven into a sort of waves: in some places the ground sunk into hollows.

Gilbert White (London)

9th 1948 75°F recorded in London suburbs, and 70°F in Hull.

10th 1891 Great blizzard across southern England. The snow was being driven by gales of such force and speed that it scarcely settled on the ground at all, but piled up vertically against any standing object. Everywhere landscapes were so trans-formed that even local people had great difficulty in finding their way about. In Tavy Cleave ravine, on the west of Dartmoor, drifts are believed to have reached almost 300 feet in depth. Half a million trees were blown down, but there was no loss of life, and one man survived by standing against a hedge, putting an overcoat over his head and stamping out a pit for his legs. Sheep gave birth to lambs in similar cocoons deep in the snow.

12th 1802 The sun shone while it rained, and the stones of the walls and the pebbles on the road glittered like silver.

Dorothy Wordsworth (Lake District)

13th 1802 After dinner we walked to Rydale for letters – it was terribly cold – we had 2 or 3 brisk hail showers – the hail stones looked clean and pretty upon the dry clean road. Little Peggy Simpson was standing at the door catching the hail stones in her hand – she grows very like her mother.

Dorothy Wordsworth (Lake District)

14th 1958 Lowest March temperature ever: -9°F at the appropriately named Logie Coldstone in Scotland.

16th 1947 Thaw floods following the long 1947 winter. Snow had fallen somewhere in Britain every day since 22 January, and the accumulation represented countless million tons of potential flood water. The thaw began sweeping across the country from 10 March with the arrival of warm, rainy Atlantic air (snow will melt at the rate of 250 mm a day under these conditions) and rivers everywhere came close to breaking their banks. In East Anglia, they did so after severe SW gales blowing along the line of the major rivers drove the high water over the dykes. In the Fens many thousands of acres were inundated, and it was June before all the land had re-emerged.

20th 1788 Violent hail-storm, which filled the gutter, and came in and flooded the stair-case; and came down the chimnies and wetted the floors.

Gilbert White (Selborne)

21st 1798 We drank tea at Coleridge's. A quiet shower of snow was in the air during more than half our walk.

Dorothy Wordsworth (Somerset)

23rd 1947 Selby in Yorks. almost completely submerged by the thaw floods. Three-quarters of all the houses were under water.

23rd 1771 Dr Johnson says '. . . the season in the Island of Sky, . . . is remembered by the name of the *black spring*. The snow, which seldom lies at all, covered the ground for eight weeks, many cattle dyed, & those that survived were so emaciated and dispirited that they did not require the male at the usual season.

Gilbert White (Selborne)

24th 1669 A mighty cold and windy but clear day and had the pleasure of seeing the Medway running, winding up and down mightily, and a very fine country.

Samuel Pepys (Kent)

March

24th 1975 Racing clouds, spring air, rooks tossing over the elms. The green bleeds in from the ground: young corn covers the fields, but the trees are still bare.

R.M. (Norfolk)

25th 1953 Thirty-fourth day without rain, the longest spring period of absolute drought since 1893.

26th/27th 1968 9.8 inches of rain over a two-day period in NW Highlands.

27th 1982 End of a week of hot, fine weather, with daytime temperatures in top 60s. Disorientating weather. Hot, still, sultry, brazen skies, but no leaves yet.

R.M. (Hants.)

29th 1929 Highest March temperature ever: 77°F in Wakefield (equalled on the same date in 1968 at several places in Norfolk).

29th 1952 Severe late snowstorm in Midlands and south produced drifts of up to 6 feet deep.

31st 1768 This day the dry weather has lasted a month.

Gilbert White (Hants.)

April

Popular Misconceptions – England

2nd 1937 First car passes over Killhope Summit in Weardale, after the head of the dale had been blocked by 12-foot deep snowdrifts for 7 weeks.

2nd 1973 An ice meteor (see p. 14) weighing between 2 and 4 lb crashed into Burton Road, Manchester. The largest remaining fragment (rushed to a deep freeze) weighed 20 ounces and was 5½ inches long.

4th 1772 Mackril sky, wheel round the sun. Clouds in horison.

Gilbert White (Selborne)

April

5th 1793   The air smells very sweet, and salubrious. Men dig their hop-gardens, and sow spring corn . . . Many flies are out basking in the sun.

Gilbert White (Selborne)

5th 1911   The largest timber tree in Britain – the wych elm in Magdalen College, Oxford, estimated to contain 2000 cubic feet of timber – blown down in a snowstorm.

8th 1979   Eleven soccer players at Caerleon, Gwent, were each struck by lightning as they ran off the field during a thunderstorm. Only one was seriously hurt.

10th 1783   Therm. 72!!! Prodigious heat: clouds of dust.

Gilbert White (South Lambeth)

11th 1979   70°F on south coast. Able to sit in garden with shirt off.

R.M. (Herts.)

16th 1949   Highest April temperature on record: 85°F in Camden Square, London.

17th 1873   Magnetic weather, sunlight soft and bright, colour of fells and fields far off seeming as if dipped in watery blue.

Gerard Manley Hopkins (Lancs.)

18th 1957   Duststorms frequent in arable areas after exceptionally dry spring, and an extreme northerly one damaged crops in the Moray Firth.

19th 1873   Entirely Paradise of a day, cloudless and pure till 5: then East wind a little, but clearing for twilight. Did little but saunter among primroses and work on beach.

John Ruskin (Lake Coniston)

20th 1771   The dry weather has lasted five weeks this day. Just rain enough to discolour the pavement.

Gilbert White (Selborne)

20th 1772   Thick ice. No swallows appear.

Gilbert White (Selborne)

23rd–26th 1908   12 inches of snow lay in parts of Norfolk and Suffolk.

24th 1981   Caught in freak sleet and hail blizzard whilst filming in Birmingham. Drainingly cold wind. The cameramen we were working with had to go inside the trailer every half-an-hour for thawing out before they could operate the equipment again. 4 inches of snow fell in parts of the city, and nationally it was the most severe April weather since 1908.

R.M. (Midlands)

26th 1950   Snow lies 6 inches deep in a belt between Wilts. and Kent.

26th 1973   Hot, hazy sun. Tar bubbles in road.

R.M. (Herts.)

28th 1775 Sun, sultry, fierce heat! Midsummer evening. The sun scorched 'til within an hour of setting.

Gilbert White (Selborne)

May

'I wish our hour was up'

1st 1796 No service at church this morning, being under repair. A most gracious rain almost the whole night. Lord make us thankfull for the same.

Parson Woodforde (Norfolk)

2nd 1979 Strong, cold NW wind. In the afternoon, a violent hailstorm with thunderclaps, the most freezing, smarting, painful I can ever remember. Rooks fled back to the trees, and clung to their nests.

R.M. (Bucks.)

6th 1957   End of 41 consecutive days without rain in the Wye valley.

7th 1979   A small waterspout, about 10 feet high, was seen offshore at Mablethorpe, Lincs., after a solitary flash of lightning. Described as resembling 'steam rising off a boiling sea'.

8th 1976   84°F at height of day at Kew Gardens.

11th 1785   Severe drying exhausting drought. Cloudless days. The country all dust.

Gilbert White (Selborne)

11th 1872   May is usually the worst and coldest month in the year but this beats them all and out-herods Herod. A black bitter wind violent and piercing drove from the East with showers of snow. The mountains and Clyro Hill and Cusop Hill were quite white with snow. The hawthorn bushes are white with may and snow at the same time.

Francis Kilvert (Radnor)

14th 1802   A very cold morning – hail and showers all day ... William tired himself with seeking an epithet for the cuckoo.

Dorothy Wordsworth (Lake District)

15th 1769   The ground dryed-up in a very extraordinary manner. Much barley lying in the dust without vegetating.

Gilbert White (Selborne)

May

15th 1893 End of the longest period of absolute drought in Britain – 73 successive days at Mile End, London.

16th 1953 A heavy, late snowfall in Lancs., following an unusual invasion of Arctic air.

16th 1980 End of 6 days of almost continuous sunshine at Kew. (97 hours, some 90 per cent of the maximum possible.)

17th 1800 Incessant rain from morning till night. T. Ashburner brought us coals. Worked hard, and read *Midsummer Night's Dream*.
Dorothy Wordsworth (Lake District)

19th 1952 A tornado in Derbyshire – small, but doing a great deal of local damage.

20th 1981 Very electric day. Great storms; charged, dizzying air.
R.M. (Herts.)

21st 1874 A mockery of bright sunshine day after day, no rain . . . wind always holding from the north, dim blue skies, faint clouds, ashy frosts in the mornings: saw young ivy leaves along the sunk fence bitten and blackened.
Gerard Manley Hopkins (Surrey)

21st 1950 The occasion of Britain's longest-lived and most substantial tornado. It originated somewhere in Berks., during a spell of very low pressure and thunderstorms on a Sunday afternoon. The funnel cloud raced north, through Puttenham in Herts., where it exploded a pig-byre and lifted a Nissen hut into a tree. Television aerials were twisted like corkscrews and some chickens plucked clean of feathers. At Leighton Buzzard in Beds., a cat was seen in full flight, with all four legs spread out in an automatic balancing act. The tornado petered out a hundred miles further north on the Norfolk coast at about 8 p.m. The wind circulation speed at its centre was estimated at 230 m.p.h.

22nd 1874   Ground parched. Then a thunderstorm, and after that the nightingales singing at night.
Gerard Manley Hopkins (Surrey)

25th 1979   The second waterspout in one month off Mablethorpe. This one rose to an estimated height of 1000 feet, and was in view for 15 minutes.

26th/27th 1775   We are obliged to water the garden continually . . . No thoro' rain in this district since the 9, 10 and 11 of March.
Gilbert White (Selborne)

26th 1978   A mirage of Hull Docks was seen on the skyline at Bridlington, 25 miles away.

29th 1944   Highest May temperature on record: 91°F at a number of places in SE England.

30th 1979   A tornado on Salisbury Plain destroyed 200 mature fir trees.

June

'I tell you, I don't like it Timothy, firstly, what's it doing up there and secondly, why is it so hot!'

1st–3rd 1947   Four successive days over 90°F in London.

2nd 1975   Snow stopped play at a game of cricket in Colchester, and also fell at Lords.

2nd 1982   A hot spell broke with great electric storms. TV reception was wiped out for most of the evening across SE England, and flash floods closed the Euston–Birmingham railway line. During storms in parts of Derbyshire 3 inches of rain fell in 20 minutes and the thunder could be heard 30 miles away.

June

3rd 1979 Bizarre, oppressive hot mist bottles up the area the whole day. Very claustrophobic.

R.M. (SW Herts.)

4th 1800 A very fine day. I sate out of doors most of the day . . . walked to the lake-side in the morning, took up plants, and sate upon a stone reading Ballads.

Dorothy Wordsworth (Lake District)

5th 1784 At noon . . . I observed a blue mist, smelling strongly of sulphur, hanging along our sloping woods, and seeming to indicate that thunder was at hand . . . It began with vast drops of rain which were soon succeeded by round hail, and then by convex pieces of ice, which measured three inches in girth . . . We were just sitting down to dinner; but were soon diverted from our repast by the clattering of tiles and the jingling of glass. . . . The hollow lane towards Alton was so torn and disordered as not to be passable till mended, rocks being removed that weighed two hundredweight. Those that saw the effect which the great hail had on ponds and pools say that the dashing of the water made an extraordinary appearance, the froth and spray standing up in the air three feet above the surface.

Gilbert White (Selborne)

6th 1975 Heat-wave begins. Temperatures had risen over 40°F since 2 June.

6th 1977 Jubilee Day ushered in by cold, blustery weather. Those celebrating at the beacon bonfires on Scafell and Skiddaw were up to their ankles in snow.

7th 1665 The hottest day that ever I felt in my life.

Samuel Pepys (London)

7th 1874 Another glowing glorious day of sunshine and unclouded blue. But every day the drought grows drier and the predicted water famine is stealing upon us.

Francis Kilvert (Wilts.)

10th 1800 Cold showers with hail and rain, but at half past five, after a heavy rain, the lake became calm and very beautiful. Those parts of the water which were perfectly unruffled lay like green islands of various shapes.

Dorothy Wordsworth (Lake District)

11th 1775 We have had an extraordinary drought, no grass, no leaves, no flowers; not a white rose for the festival of yesterday! About four arrived such a flood, that we could not see out of the windows: the whole lawn was a lake, though situated on so high an Ararat . . . It never came into my head before, that a rainbow-office for insuring against water might be very necessary.

Horace Walpole (Middlesex)

11th 1956 6.1 inches of rain fell on Hewenden Reservoir, Yorkshire, over a period of 2 hours.

12th 1791 Snow fell in London, but melted as soon as it reached the ground.

13th 1783   The sun continues to rise and set without his rays, and hardly shines at noon. At eleven last night the moon was a dull red; she was nearly at her highest elevation, and had the colour of heated brick.

William Cowper (Bucks.)

14th 1791   It froze hard last night: I went out for a moment to look at my haymakers, and was starved. The contents of an English June are hay and ice, orange flowers and rheumatism. I am now cowering near the fire.

Horace Walpole (Middlesex)

15th 1775   Tremendous thunder, and vast hail yesterday at Bramshot, and Hedley with prodigious floods. Vast damage done. The hail lay knee-deep.

Gilbert White (Selborne)

17th 1976   3.26 inches of rain fell on Cambridge in 2 hours.

18th 1785   After an exceptionally severe spring, snowdrifts were still lingering in the Lake District.

18th 1982   Freak storms in Bristol. Hailstones fell so thick and fast that in places they drifted to a depth of 2 feet.

19th 1799   Very cold indeed again today, so cold that Mrs Custance came walking in her spencer with a bosom-friend.

Parson Woodforde (Norfolk)

21st 1977   No sun recorded at Kew since 17 June, longest June sunless spell there since records began.

23rd 1783   The peculiar haze, or smokey fog, that prevailed for many weeks in this island, and in every part of Europe, and even beyond its limits, was a most extraordinary appearance, unlike anything known within the memory of man. By my journal I find that I had noticed this strange occurrence from June 23 to July 20 inclusive, during which period the wind varied to every quarter without making any alteration in the air. The sun, at noon, looked as blank as a clouded moon, and shed a rust-coloured ferruginous light on the ground, and floors of rooms; but was particularly lurid and blood-coloured at rising and setting. All the time the heat was so intense that butcher's meat could hardly be eaten on the day after it was killed; and the flies swarmed so in the lanes and hedges that they rendered the horses half frantic, and riding irksome. The country people began to look with a superstitious awe, at the red, louring aspect of the sun.

Gilbert White (Selborne)

25th 1771   Rain-bow. Rock-like clouds. Sweet evening. Moonshine.

Gilbert White (Selborne)

25th 1976   Heat-wave well established, with temperatures in the 90s. When a train was stranded for 90 minutes in the London underground passengers broke windows to get air.

26th 1976 110°F on the Centre Court at Wimbledon. 400 spectators faint.

26th 1980 Hail stops play at Wimbledon.

27th 1974 A bizarre natural disaster at Tring Reservoirs, Herts. A hot month had encouraged a dense layer of bright green algae to grow over the surface of one of the reservoirs. Then a sudden overnight downpour of very cold rain caused a temperature inversion: the cooled surface (plus weed) sank to the bottom, where most of the fish were feeding and resting. Plants absorb oxygen in the dark, and the arrival of this mass of waterweed had the effect of suffocating the bottom-feeding fish. The next morning many thousands were found floating dead upon the surface.

28th 1917 Heaviest rainfall for a day: 9.56 inches at Bruton in Somerset.

29th 1957 Highest June temperature – 96°F – recorded in Camden Square, London. (Equalled in Southampton on 28 June 1976.)

30th 1866 Thunderstorms all day, great claps and lightning running up and down. When it was bright between times great towering clouds behind which the sun put out his shaded horns very clearly and a longish way. Level curds and whey sky after sunset.
Gerard Manley Hopkins (Oxford)

30th 1975 A whirlwind at Bristol. The whirlwind appeared as a dark column of spinning air as it travelled. It lifted a shed off its supports and landed it on a car in the car park about 60 yards away.

July

Percy. *'Does it always rain in this ghastly place?'*
Boatman. *'Lor' bless yer, no, sir. Why, only last summer
a London gent went 'ome with sunstroke'*

1st 1968 A day of extraordinary weather phenomena. 1.4 inches of rain fell in 8½ minutes at Leeming in Yorkshire; at Slapton in Devon there were hailstones 2¾ inches wide; in the west and Midlands there were severe thunderstorms, and in the southeast the temperature exceeded 90°F in many places. To cap it all, the hot North African airstream that was partly responsible for the mayhem, brought with it thousands of tons of orange desert dust which covered cars, pavements and washing.

1st 1980 Filming in Upper Teesdale, Durham. Holed up in a barn by driving rain and freezing winds. So cold that we had to play cricket to keep warm, with a shepherd's crook and a ball made up of electrician's tape.

R.M. (Durham)

2nd 1980 Wimbledon. Billy Jean King and Chris Lloyd's semifinal dramatically interrupted at 'deuce' after 'match point' by a sudden torrential downpour. There was only one day's play without some rain this year, and the centre court's new computerized scoreboard was kept busy amusing the drenched crowd by printing out jokes, and the words for community singing. (The chances of rain preventing play altogether at Wimbledon are quite small. Just three afternoons have been missed out of the last 205.)

4th 1802 Cold and rain and very dark. I was sick and ill, had been made sleepless by letters.

Dorothy Wordsworth (Lake District)

5th 1963 A downpour over Hemyock in Devon produced 1 inches of rain in 15 minutes and 3.1 inches in 1¼ hours.

8th 1871 There was this day a thunderstorm on a greater scale – huge rocky clouds lit with livid light, hail and rain that flooded the garden, and thunder ringing and echoing like brass.

Gerard Manley Hopkins (Lancs.)

9th 1981 3.1 inches of rain fell in 70 minutes at Littleover, Derbyshire.

11th 1888 Sleet fell in many places in England as far south as Kent.

11th 1965 Rain fell for 70 hours without break in Cardiff.

11th 1783 The heat overcomes the grass mowers and makes them sick. There was not rain enough in the village to lay the dust.

Gilbert White (Selborne)

12th 1900 3.75 inches of rain fell on Ilkley, Yorks., in 1¼ hours.

13th 1667 Mighty hot weather, I lying this night, which I have not done, I believe, since a boy, with only a rug and sheet upon me.

Samuel Pepys (London)

16th 1666 A wonderful dark sky and shower of rain this morning. At Harwich a shower of hail as big as walnuts.

Samuel Pepys (Essex)

18th 1772 Frequent sprinklings, but not enough all day to lay the dust. The dry fit has lasted six weeks this day.

Gilbert White (Selborne)

18th 1812 Snow persists on Helvellyn. (There is nowhere in England where snow lies the whole year.)

18th 1964 2.2 inches of rain fell in 15 minutes in Bolton.

July

18th/19th 1955   11 inches of rain fell over 15 hours in Martinstown, Dorset. This is the record for a 24-hour period.

19th 1803   Intensely hot day – left off waistcoat, and for yarn wore silk stockings.
> Samuel Coleridge (Lake District)

20th/23rd 1930   Continuous rain for three days in the north. 12 inches fell on Castleton in the Yorkshire moors.

21st 1965   The Wisley Tornado. At about 3 p.m. a whirlwind cut a swathe between 10 and 30 metres wide through the Royal Horticultural Society Gardens, uprooting orchard trees and splitting other trees up to 3 metres in girth. The whole tornado lasted only 10 minutes.

22nd 1868   100.5°F at Tonbridge, the highest air temperature ever recorded in Britain.

22nd 1873   Very hot, though the wind, which was south, dappled very sweetly on one's face and when I came out I seemed to put it on like a gown. I mean it rippled and fluttered like light linen, one could feel the folds and braids of it.
> Gerard Manley Hopkins (Surrey)

23rd 1800   It was excessively hot, but the day after, Friday 24 July, still hotter. All the morning I was engaged in unpacking our Somersetshire goods and in making pies. The house was a hot oven, but yet we could not bake the pies. I was so weary, I could not walk.

Dorothy Wordsworth (Lake District)

26th 1802 The clouds were scattered by wind and rain in all shapes and heights, above the mountains, on their sides, and low down to their bases – some masses in the middle of the valley – when the wind and rain dropt down and died, and for two hours all the clouds, white and fleecy all of them, remained without motion, forming an appearance not very unlike the moon as seen thro' a telescope . . . I have often thought of writing a set of play-bills for the Vale of Keswick – for every day in the year – announcing each day the performance, by his supreme Majesty's Servants, Clouds, Water, Sun, Moon, Stars, etc.

Samuel Coleridge (Lake District)

29th 1948 Temperatures over 90°F recorded as far north as Prestwick, during a nationwide heat-wave.

29th 1777 . . . such vast rains fell about Iping, Bramshot, Haselmere, etc, that they tore vast holes in the turnpike roads, covered several meadows with sand and silt, blowed-up the heads of several ponds, carryed away part of the country-bridge at Iping, and the garden-walls of the paper mill . . .

Gilbert White (Selborne)

August

'*The beach, with its thousands of happy faces, presented an animated scene.*' – Any Press report from Anywhere-on-Sea

3rd 1782   Our meadows are covered with a winter-flood in August; the rushes with which our bottom-less chairs were to have been bottomed, and much hay which was not carried, are gone down the river on a voyage to Ely, and it is even uncertain whether they will ever return.

William Cowper (Bucks.)

6th 1956   Hailstones drifted to a depth of 4 feet in Tonbridge Wells. In Arundel, where they lay 2 feet deep, they were swept aside onto a roadside verge under dense tree cover, and survived unmelted for 3 days, despite temperatures in the 70s.

6th 1981   A severe storm in London during the evening rush hour. 1.9 inches of rain fell in 3 hours.

7th 1980   Blakeney. Terrible black sky and smoky atmosphere in late afternoon unleashes fierce storm. 4½ inches of rain in 4 hours. The hotel fire-alarm set off every time lightning flashed nearby.

R.M. (Norfolk)

8th 1975   The fifth day in succession with temperatures over 90°F in southern England was interrupted by violent thunderstorms. An electricity sub-station in Bradford-on-Avon was set on fire after being struck by lightning.

9th 1911   Highest August temperature on record and the highest temperature recorded this century: 98.8°F at Ponders End, London.

10th 1871   (St Lawrence's Day) Tonight was the great August meteor shower and Uncle Will and I went up to the gate to watch for the meteors which the Irish call 'St Lawrence's tears'.

Francis Kilvert (Wilts.)

10th 1975   At Berwick-on-Tweed a cricket umpire was struck by lightning which welded solid an iron joint in his leg.

12th 1948 Flash-floodwater pouring off the Lammermuir Hills, Berwickshire, destroyed seven main-line railway bridges over the River Eye. Roads were blocked by landslides, and hundreds of acres of farmland were buried under a pall of mud and rocks 6 feet deep.

13th 1872 Entirely calm and clear morning. The mist from the river at rest among the trees, with rosy light on its folds of blue; and I, for the first time these ten years, happy.

John Ruskin (Berks.)

13th/14th 1979 The Fastnet yacht disaster. Unexpected hurricane-force winds caused waves up to 44 feet high. Fifteen yachtsmen were drowned and twenty-four boats sunk or abandoned.

14th 1979 As the Fastnet storm was moving up the Irish Sea, a rainbow was observed off Llandudno that lasted for an exceptional 3 hours.

14th 1975 The Great Hampstead storm. In the midst of the heat-wave there was an intense local build-up of cumulus cloud over the hilly ground of northwest London. Seeded by city dust particles carried upwards by the hot air currents, it broke at 5.25 p.m. in an unprecedented deluge of three-quarter-inch-wide hailstones and monsoon rain. (I was on the phone to a friend in the area at the moment the storm broke, and could hear the rain and hail crashing onto the windows. It sounded as if they were drilling in the road.) Within 5 minutes of the start of the storm most homes in Haverstock Hill were under 5 feet of water, and floodwater was pouring into local underground stations. The storm lasted less than 3 hours and was very localized (Holborn, just two miles to the south, had 0.2 inches of rain) but during that time 6.72 inches fell on a strip about 4 miles long by 2 miles wide centred on Hampstead. One man died in a flooded basement flat, more than 400 homes were damaged and there were enormous traffic jams, way beyond the deluge, because pressure on the storm drains forced manhole covers open. One indirect casualty was the evening's Promenade Concert. The principal instrumentalists were held up in the jams and the start had to be delayed by half an hour.

15th 1952   8.9 inches of rain fell on Longstone Barrow on Exmoor. This West Country deluge will always be remembered because of the terrible flooding of Lynmouth that followed. The month had already been exceptionally wet, and the Exmoor peat was unable to absorb the vast extra quantities of water. The East and West Lyn rivers broke their dams and banks and surged down into the little seaside town of Lynmouth carrying with them 200,000 tons of boulders and trees. Houses, hotels and cars were washed away (thirty-eight of the latter never to be found again) and thirty-four lives were lost. During the mammoth rescue and rehabilitation job outsiders were excluded from the town until 2 September.

15th 1772   On this day at 10 in the morning some sober and intelligent people felt at Noar hill what they thought to be a slight shock of an earthquake.

A mother and her son perceived the house to tremble at the same time while one was above stairs and the other below; and each called to the other to know what was the matter.

Gilbert White (Selborne)

16/18th 1924 9½ inches of rain fell over a 25-hour period at Cannington in Somerset.

18th 1974 Many waterspouts sighted in the Channel, between Hants. and Sussex. One report described 'six spouts in a U-shape curved round the yacht, distance 2½–4 miles. There was a solid fountain of spray, 300 feet high and 150 feet wide, with nil visibility. The spouts lasted 10–20 minutes and then dissipated. Lightning and thunder were occurring at the same time'.

22nd 1975 A waterspout off Kessingland, Norfolk, struck inland, ripping tiles and guttering off houses on the coastline.

23rd 1855 I have been, in the dusk of the evening, taking a walk along Pevensey Level – a quiet, broad, seaside road; the wind soft and cool; the sky orange, most soft in the west, but with leaden, purple, ragged clouds floating here and there in masses and wild flakes about the sky, and dragging streaks of rain across the darkening downs. In the east, a large, rose-coloured, steadfast cloud arising from fresh blue-grey banks of sinking nimbi, with the summer lightning incessantly fluttering in its bosom, like thoughts.

James Smetham (Sussex)

25th 1860   Tintagel: Black cliffs and caves and storm and wind, but I weather it out and take my ten miles a day walks in my weather-proofs.

Alfred, Lord Tennyson (Cornwall)

25th/26th 1912   Severe floods in East Anglia. In Norwich 7.3 inches of rain (three times the monthly average) fell in less than 24 hours. The River Wensum was turned into a torrent which raced through the centre of the city, destroying almost all the bridges.

26th 1977   River Isis in flood after 5 days torrential rain, and punts cannot get upstream.

R.M. (Oxford)

27th 1981   Another beautiful day, clearer, hotter even than yesterday. This is the twentieth day of hot sunshine this month. Walked along the River Chess at Chenies and found people in a festive mood, looking relaxed, accessible, talking to each other and to strangers. Such wonders the sun does!

R.M. (Chilterns)

29th 1936   The greatest daily range in temperature in Britain was recorded in a frost-hollow near Rickmansworth, on the edge of the Chilterns: 34°F at 6 a.m. and 84.9° at 2 p.m. (The hollow is a steep, narrow combe on the chalk, notorious for exceptional and unseasonable temperatures. Dahlias are regularly lost here in August.)

29th 1976 End of what is believed to be the most severe drought in England and Wales for 1000 years. The hot weather began in mid-June and in eastern England the average daily sunshine was over 10 hours for two months on end. Rainfall at Kew for June, July and August was 46 mm, which is about a quarter of the average. But the areas worst hit were in the West. Many reservoirs were losing water by evaporation at the rate of 5.5 million gallons a day, and some dried out completely until their mud bases cracked. The impact of the drought on water supplies was especially serious as it had come at the end of four exceptionally dry years, and in Wales, one million people were forced to use standpipes for nearly eleven weeks. In the countryside field and stubble fires were rampant and pastures parched so brown as to be useless to cattle. Many trees shed their leaves to conserve their water supplies (and were unfortunately mistaken for dead). But in general living things – including the human population – adapted remarkably well. Dress habits changed dramatically, and shorts for men became commonplace, even for work. Restaurants put out tables on the pavements and the whole country slid with an ease that surprised many into a festive and relaxed Mediterranean lifestyle. It was only during the periods of exceptionally high temperatures that the inexperience of the British in coping with heat became obvious in outbreaks of food poisoning, sunstroke, exhaustion and general bad temper. The drought ended with downpours on the 29th, and September proved to be one of the wettest on record with double the average rainfall. Denis Howell, who had been appointed Minister for Drought, had rapidly to change his remit, and thereafter became Minister for all kinds of in-temperate weather.

September

'I expect you heard the disastrous news about the cricket, dear'

1st–3rd 1906 Daytime temperatures remain above 90°F for 4 days. On the 2nd, 96°F was recorded at Barnet, Epsom and Bawtry (N. Yorks.) – the highest September temperature on record.

1st 1823 From Tenterden I set off at five o'clock, and got to Appledore after a most delightful ride, the high land upon my right, and the low land upon my left. The fog was so thick and white along some of the low land, that I should have taken it for water, if little hills and trees had not risen up through it here and there.

William Cobbett (Kent)

4th–6th 1951   Spectacular display of the aurora borealis visible at night over the whole of England.

5th 1958   The heaviest recorded hailstone in Britain fell at Horsham in Sussex. It weighed 5 ounces. An eye-witness account of the storm described how at Hillsgreen Farm '10,000 bushels of apples from 50 acres were destroyed, the remainder left on the trees were nearly all hail-marked and worthless ... There were also reports of small pits left in lawns where hailstones had melted.'

11th 1978   A whirlwind formed when two stubble fires met in a field at Climping, Sussex. It travelled 200 yards carrying glowing cinders which set fire to and destroyed four thatched cottages.

12th 1975   Strange March-like weather. Brilliant early mornings, dew-sharp; then blustering winds, racing clouds, short showers.

R.M. (Herts.)

14th 1777   A tremendous and awful earthquake at Manchester, and the district round. The earthquake happened a little before eleven o' the clock in the forenoon, when many of the inhabitants were assembled at their respective places of worship.

Gilbert White (Selborne)

14th 1873   ... one of the loveliest mornings that ever dawned upon this world. A heavy dew had fallen in the night and as I wandered down the beautiful winding terraced walks every touch sent a shower from the great blue globes of the hydrangeas, and on every crimson fuchsia pendant flashed a diamond dew drop.

The clear pure crisp air of the early morning blew fresh and exhilarating as the breeze came sweet from the sea.

Francis Kilvert (Devon)

15th 1785 The dripping weather has lasted *this day nine weeks*, all thro' haying & harvest.

Gilbert White (Selborne)

16th 1968 The River Mole floods, and devastates thousands of homes in Molesey, Cobham and Sunbury.

17th 1777 The creeping fogs in the pastures are very picturesque and amusing and represent arms of the sea, rivers, and lakes.

Gilbert White (Selborne)

17th 1961 Remnants of Hurricane Debbie hit the western Scottish coast, bringing gusts up to 88 m.p.h.

18th 1796 What dreadful hot weather we have! – It keeps one in a continual state of inelegance.

Jane Austen (Kent)

22nd 1783 Thunder: rather the guns at Portsmouth. Splendid rain-bow. After three weeks wet, this rainbow preceded (as I have often known before) a lovely fit of weather.

Gilbert White (Selborne)

23rd 1783 Black snails lie out, and copulate. Vast swagging clouds.

Gilbert White (Selborne)

24th 1870 First saw the Northern Lights. My eye was caught by beams of light and dark very like the crown of horny rays the sun makes behind a cloud. At first I thought of silvery cloud until I saw that these were more luminous and did not dim the clearness of the stars in the Bear. They rose slightly radiating thrown out from the earthline. Then I saw soft pulses of light one after another rise and pass upwards arched in shape but waveringly and with the arch broken. They seemed to float, not following the warp of the sphere as falling stars look to do but free though concentrical with it.

Gerard Manley Hopkins (Lancs.)

25th 1885 Earliest recorded snowfall in London.

25th 1780 When people walk in a deep white fog by night with a lanthorn, if they will turn their backs to the light they will see their shades impressed on the fog in rude, gigantic proportions. This phenomenon seems not to have been attended to; but implies the great intensity of the meteor of that juncture.

Gilbert White (Selborne)

26th 1971 A tornado in Rotherham, Yorks., moved a 90-ton locomotive 50 yards along the track. In nearby Rawmarsh there were reports of an Alsatian in its kennel being blown over a fence and of garden railings being sucked out of the ground.

October

'Right! Now I want each of you to describe the weather in your own words'

1st 1800 A fine morning, a showery night. The lake still in the morning; in the forenoon flashing light from the beams of the sun, as it was ruffled by the wind.

> Dorothy Wordsworth (Grasmere)

2nd 1800 A very rainy morning. We walked after dinner to observe the torrents.

> Dorothy Wordsworth (Lake District)

2nd 1980 An ice meteor crashed through the roof of a house in Plymouth.

October

6th 1921 Highest October temperature on record: 84°F in London.

9th 1871 There was a frost in the night and this morning the tops of the poplar spires are touched, are turned to finest gold.

Francis Kilvert (Radnorshire)

9th 1800 Very rainy. Wm and I walked in the evening . . . but it came on so very rainy that we were obliged to shelter at Fleming's. A grand Ball at Rydale. After sitting some time we went homewards and were again caught by a shower and sheltered under the sycamores at the boat-house – very cold snowlike rain.

Dorothy Wordsworth (Grasmere)

10th 1959 End of 57 days of drought in Lowestoft, Suffolk.

11th–14th 1786 The news papers mention vast floods about the country; and that much damage has been done by high tides, and tempestuous winds . . . The hop-planters of this parish returned from Wey-hill fair with chearful faces and full purses; having sold large crop of hops for a good price. The hops of Kent were blown away by the storms, after the crop of this country was gathered in.

Gilbert White (Selborne)

15th 1670 Lightning strikes twice in the same place. On the 15th July 1670, the church of St Mary in Steeple Ashton, Wilts., was cracked by lightning. Repair work was started at once, and was almost complete when lightning struck again on 15 October. This time the steeple collapsed completely, killing two workmen and crashing into the main body of the church – which took another 5 years to repair.

17th 1091 A tornado struck in London, lifting off the roof of the church of St Mary-le-Bow. Four rafters, 26 feet long, were driven into the ground with such force that only 4 feet protruded above ground.

20th 1802 A windy, showery day – with great columns of misty sunshine travelling along the lake toward Borrodale, the heavens a confusion of white clouds in masses, and bright blue sky.

Samuel Coleridge (Lake District)

20th 1950 Exceptionally early cold weather. 12°F of air frost on Salisbury Plain.

21st 1638 The parish church at Widecombe-in-the-moor in Devon was struck by massive tornado during morning service. The church roof fell in and four of the congregation were killed. Others were burned or had their clothes ripped off, and one man found the money in his purse partly melted.

22nd 1801 Thursday evening, ½ past 6. All the mountains black and tremendously obscure, except Swinside . . . At this time I saw one after the other, nearly in the same place, two perfect Moon Rainbows.

Samuel Coleridge (Lake District)

October

23rd 1954 Heavy rains cause a landslide in Nant Ffrancon pass on the Holyhead Road.

29th 1873 Wonderful downpouring of leaf: when the morning sun began to melt the frost they fell at one touch and in a few minutes a whole tree was flung of them; they lay masking and papering the ground at its foot.

Gerard Manley Hopkins (Surrey)

31st 1976 The worst drought in 1000 years followed by the wettest October for 70 years.

November

Obliging Driver (to country visitor in intense fog): 'That there's the Halbert Memorial, but you can't see it!'

1st 1771 An imperfect rainbow on the fog; a more vivid one on the dewy grass.

Gilbert White (Selborne)

3rd 1770 Misling rain all day.

Gilbert White (Selborne)

4th 1946 Highest November temperature on record: 71°F at Prestatyn.

4th 1957 Twenty-four houses on a new estate in Hatfield, Herts., built with experimental low-pitch aluminium roofs, were stripped of their roofs during locally gusting gales.

4th 1800 W[illiam] went to the Tarn, afterwards to the top of Seat Sandal. He was obliged to lie down in the tremendous wind. The snow blew from Helvellyn horizontally like smoke.

Dorothy Wordsworth (Lake District)

5th 1938 70°F in Cambridge.

7th 1980 Exceptionally cold. Snow falls in southeast England. The early wintery weather believed to be due to the eruption of the Mount St Helen volcano, and the subsequent spreading of millions of tons of ash into the upper atmosphere.

10th 1803 Thursday night, ¼ after 7. The sky covered with stars; the wind up; right opposite my window, over Brandelhow ... an enormous black cloud exactly in the shape of an egg – this the only cloud in all the sky – impressed me with a daemonical grandeur.

Samuel Coleridge (Lake District)

13th 1801 Dullish, damp and cloudy – a day that promises not to dry our clothes.

Dorothy Wordsworth (Lake District)

13th 1872 The first frost of autumn. Outdoor folk look reflective.

Thomas Hardy (Dorset)

14th 1786 Boys slide on the Ice!

Gilbert White (Selborne)

November

19th 1771 Solway Moss Floods. On 14 November 1771, heavy rain inundated the north of England, and by the 19th the River Tees had risen 20 feet. North of Carlisle, the bog known as Solway Moss had soaked up such a prodigious quantity of water that the peat swelled sufficiently to breach the solid earth shell which capped and retained it. Peat, mud and wet sphagnum moss poured into the valley and formed a quagmire a mile across. Many cattle and sheep were suffocated and 900 acres of farmland were left covered in the debris up to a depth of 20 feet.

19th 1776 This afternoon the weather turning suddenly very warm produced an unusual appearance; for the dew on the windows was on the *outside* of the glass, the air being warmer *abroad* than *within*.
Gilbert White (Selborne)

19th 1851 Fearfully cold. Landscape trees upon my window-panes. After breakfast chopped wood, and after that painted ivy.
John Everett Millais (Surrey)

19th–28th 1936 Continuous thick fog in Manchester, with visibility below 220 yards for almost the whole period.

22nd 1788 The smoke of the new lighted lime-kilns this evening crept along the ground in long trails: a token of a dry, heavy atmosphere.
Gilbert White (Selborne)

November

24th 1801 Moonlight, but it rained. I met [William] before I had got as far as John Baty's – he had been surprised and terrified by a sudden rushing of winds which served to bring earth, sky and lake together, as if the whole were going to enclose him in; he was glad he was in a high road.

Dorothy Wordsworth (Lake District)

26th/27th 1703 The worst storm ever documented for the British Isles. (It was described in detail by Daniel Defoe, who was living in London at the time.) SW gales blew across southern England for 15 hours, probably exceeding hurricane strength (74 m.p.h.) continuously for more than two hours. 8000 lives were lost, mainly at sea. The Eddystone lighthouse vanished altogether. Inland, 100 churches were stripped of lead, 400 windmills blown over, and hundreds of houses completely destroyed. Defoe noted 17,000 trees uprooted in Kent before he gave up counting.

28th/29th 1979 Yellow dust from the Sahara fell on Ireland and Scotland. One scientist estimated that 60,000 tons fell on Cork alone.

29th 1938 A mean wind speed of 59 m.p.h. recorded over an hour at Cardington, Beds.

30th 1971 The M1 pile-up disaster. An early-morning fog near Luton had cleared sufficiently for car warning lights to be switched off and the sun was bright enough for many drivers to be wearing sunglasses. Then a dense patch of fog which had been lying over an adjacent field lifted in response

to the sunshine, and drifted across the motorway
. . . The result was a horrific pile-up of some eighty
vehicles across both carriageways. Seven people
were killed and forty-five injured.

December

Skating by torchlight on the Serpentine

1st 1890 Towards dark, a colourless fog, snow almost gone, and ground soft-oozy underfoot, as though the earth's skin slipped as you trod. A very dark night: no wind; church bells dinning, and myself chilly and afraid of the misty evening.

George Sturt (Surrey)

1st 1948 End of 114 hours of continuous fog in London.

1st 1966 26 tornadoes recorded for a single day.

December

2nd 1948 Highest December temperature on record: 65°F at Achnashellach.

2nd 1768 Thunder and hail. Incredible quantities of rain have fallen this week.

Gilbert White (Selborne)

1st/2nd 1975 Seven tornadoes occurred overnight in East Anglia. Turnips were sucked out of the ground in places.

3rd 1789 Beautiful picturesque, partial fogs along the vales, representing rivers, islands, and arms of the sea! These fogs in London and other parts were so deep that much mischief was occasioned by men falling into rivers and being overturned into ditches . . .

Gilbert White (Selborne)

5th 1952 The infamous London smog began. It lasted for 4 days during which the temperature in the Thames valley never rose above freezing point. Some 4000 people are believed to have died from bronchial troubles aggravated by the fatal combination of soot, sulphur dioxide and cold.

8th 1954 A tornado in West London wrecked Gunnersbury tube station, and at nearby Acton sucked a car 5 metres into the air.

9th 1981 The annual Varsity rugby match at Twickenham played with mad gallantry in 4 inches of snow at a temperature of about 20°F.

10th 1784 On Friday, being bright sun-shine, the air was full of icy *spiculae*, floating in all directions, like atoms in a sun-beam let into a dark room . . . Were they watery particles of the air frozen as they floated; or were they evaporations from the snow frozen as they mounted?

Gilbert White (Selborne)

10th 1982 The London-Southampton express derailed near Fleet by the tops of pine trees blown onto the tracks.

11th 1855 This has been a foggy morning and fore-noon, snowing a little now and then . . . At about twelve there is a faint glow of sunlight, like the gleaming reflection from a not highly polished cop-per kettle.

Nathaniel Hawthorne (Lancs.)

12th 1801 A fine frosty morning – Snow upon the ground . . . We played at cards – sate up late. The moon shone upon the water below Silver-How, and above it hung, combining with Silver-How on one side, a bowl-shaped moon, the curve downwards; the white fields, glittering roof of Thomas Ash-burner's house, the dark yew tree, the white fields gay and beautiful. Wm. lay with his curtains open that he might see it.

Dorothy Wordsworth (Lake District)

12th 1981 Frozen snow stacked up on branches and twigs, 6 inches deep. Distant woods wink and glitter in the sun at midday.

R.M. (Herts.)

December

13th 1775 Ice bears: boys slide.

Gilbert White (Selborne)

13th 1981 Heavy snow. Salt frozen in hoppers in many places. On Salisbury Plain a number of motorists were trapped in their cars on the A303 for nearly 18 hours. The snow was falling and drifting so fast on a steep, hedged section of the road that by the time the drivers had realized what was happening they were unable to open their car doors.

16th 1981 A day of storms and hurricane-force winds in England.

21st 1776 The shortest day: a truly black, and dismal one.

Gilbert White (Selborne)

23rd 1871 ½ past 9 morning. Since the morning of the 21st, the fog has never once broken, and now is intense yellow black, the room being in pure night effect, with three candles. As the clock struck 10, the gardeners could not see to work.

John Ruskin (Surrey)

25th 1870 Intense frost. I sat down in my bath upon a sheet of thick ice which broke in the middle into large pieces whilst sharp points and jagged edges stuck all round the sides of the tub like chevaux de frise, not particularly comforting to the naked thighs.

Francis Kilvert (Radnor)

December

25th 1979 Exquisite bright, clear, crisp day. Hoar frost lasting till noon. Steam rising off the top of fences, against the sun.

R.M. (Herts.)

24–27th 1927 The Christmas Blizzard. On Salisbury Plain drifts reached 20 feet, and round Alton, in Hants., 16 feet. The clouds of snow blowing out to sea from the cliffs of Devon and Dorset were so dense that passing ships mistook them for fog.

26th 1962 Heavy Boxing Day snowfalls marked the start of the 1962/63 winter, widely believed to be the worst since 1740 in its combination of snow and prolonged low temperatures. The falls on the 26th were followed by much heavier blizzards on the 29th and many towns and villages were isolated. At the beginning of January freezing rain and further heavy snowfalls ushered in a long period of severe frost, which persisted, despite many days of absolutely clear skies, until 6 March. Most places in Britain had an average of 60 days snow cover, and at Tredegar the depth throughout January was never less than 30 inches. There was a severe frost every night in most places, and even Kew experienced 13 'ice-days' when the ground temperature failed to rise above freezing point all day.

The effect of the severe cold on wildlife was catastrophic, birds particularly being unable to obtain food from the iron-hard ground. Wrens were reduced to one tenth of their usual populations, and forty-two roosted together for warmth in a single nest-box in Norfolk. In Leicestershire, a woman carrying bread rolls in an open basket was attacked and knocked down by pigeons. Another woman in the New Forest was attacked by starving ponies outside her caravan. In Northumberland sheep were seen eating the wool off each others' backs.

27th 1836 The Lewes Avalanche. Blizzards had been raging across the south of England since Christmas Eve, and gale-force easterly winds began to eddy over the lip of a 200-foot chalk precipice (once the face of a quarry) at the eastern end of Lewes. Soon a huge cornice of frozen snow built up, overhanging the row of houses at the foot of the cliff. Bright sunshine on the 27th caused the cornice to split and break away in two separate avalanches. When the major block of snow hit the ground, it exploded because of the compression of the air pockets between the ice, lifting the houses several feet off the ground, and then burying them. Eight people were killed.

27th 1981 A slight thaw produces a new, typically twentieth-century weather hazard: blocks of melting ice falling from motorway bridges through car windscreens.

27th 1768 Weather more like April than ye end of December. Hedge-sparrow sings.
>   Gilbert White (Selborne)

30th 1739 Gale-force winds across England with temperatures below 15°F.

31st 1962 7 miles of foreshore at Southend frozen, with ice stretching 200 yards out to sea.